The Sewing Lesson

Deana Sobel Lederman

TBR Books
New York

For my father

Copyright ©2020
CALEC
ISBN 978-1-947626-52-2
Library of Congress 2020940325

I was supposed
to be asleep,
but there was a light on
somewhere.

I crept out of bed
and tiptoed down the hallway.
I saw Mama sitting,
leaning over the dining room table,
her shoulders hunched up like mountains.
I heard a hummming,
tap-tap-tapping sound.

"What's that?" I asked,
wrapping an arm around her neck.

"It's a sewing machine," said Mama.

"What are you doing?" I said.

"Making masks," she said.

"What for?"

"For the people who are helping."

"Like the doctors, nurses, and other people who work at the hospital?"

Mama nodded.

"And the grocery store workers?"

Mamma nodded again.

"And our postman, and the farm workers, and . . ."

"All the people who have to work outside their homes right now," said Mama.

"How can you make so many, Mama?"

"I can't, but I can do my part."

"Can I do one?"

"Not tonight," said Mama.

Mama tucked me back into bed.

In the morning, Mama showed me
a little mask she had made just for me.
It was scritchy and scratchy,
and I didn't want to wear it at first.
I thought I looked funny, too.

But Mama put on hers,
so I put on mine,
and we went outside
to take a walk
around the park.

It was spring
and all the trees were
pinks and purples.
They reminded me of
the color of my mask.
I had almost forgotten
I was wearing it!

"When can I have my
sewing lesson?" I asked.

"No time like the present,"
said Mama.

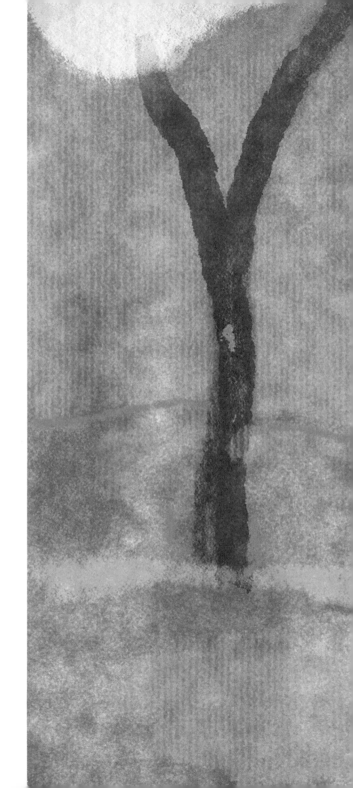

At the dining room table,
Mama taught me how to sew.
She helped me make a special mask,
just in time for a knock at the door.

It was Grandpa, just getting home from his long shift at the hospital.
I showed him the new mask I had made just for him.

He was so proud.
Oh, he was so proud!

Deana Sobel Lederman

Deana Sobel Lederman is an author, illustrator and cartoonist. Deana's grandmother was a painter who studied at The Art Students League of New York. She taught Deana to paint with oils when she was very young, and her mother always encouraged her art. Deana drew her first cartoon, The Wacky Couples, at the age of eight and went on to become the cartoonist for UC Berkeley's student newspaper, and later a freelance illustrator and cartoonist. Later, she went to law school, where she studied copyright and patent law. Deana has lived in New York City; Mill Valley and Berkeley, California; London, England; and Cambridge, Massachusetts. She lives now in San Diego, California, where she grew up, with her brilliant husband and two little boys.

TBR Books is the publishing arm of the Center for the Advancement of Languages, Education, and Communities (CALEC), a nonprofit organization with a focus on multilingualism, cross-cultural understanding, and the dissemination of ideas. Our mission is to empower multilingual families and linguistic communities through education, knowledge, and advocacy. Visit us at www.calec.org

CPSIA information can be obtained
at www.ICGtesting.com
Printed in the USA
LVHW072014010920
664636LV00013B/701